iDoodle

I0547450

iDoodle

WORD DOODLES

by

Diane Marquart Moore

Copyright © 2020 Diane Marquart Moore

Border Press
PO Box 3124
Sewanee, Tennessee 37375
www.borderpressbooks.com
victoria@borderpressbooks.com

ISBN: 978-1-7346802-2-5

Library of Congress Control Number: 2020943112

Cover image by Diane Marquart Moore

Cover and book design by Victoria Sullivan

Printed in the United States

"One thing I started learning recently is...
How to be a good listener and doodling."
- Aanchal Kharwar -

FOR VICKIE WHO NAMED THIS BOOK

INTRODUCTION

A few years ago I wrote a blog about doodling and featured the drawing now on the cover of this book. The blog explained that doodling often reinforces ideas, has an effect on memory retention, helps the brain to focus, and actually keeps minds from wandering. It's an activity that cannot be interpreted as a meaningless exercise.

Although I know one picture is worth a thousand words, I've discovered that word doodling is noteworthy and is just as satisfying as drawing doodling. Word doodles help process what's going on around a person and often present a humorous viewpoint to a serious subject, sorta' like Jewish jokes and stories.

The word doodles in this volume may not rival a drawing doodle; e.g., the visualization of prime numbers that Stanislaus Ulam created in a mathematical doodle, but there are a few doodles in *iDoodle* that could be interpreted as wisdom clothed in irony.

By reading these word doodles you may be inspired to create your own doodles, so don't dawdle, which, by the way, isn' t a form of doodling.

— Diane Marquart Moore —
Sewanee, Tennessee
July, 2020

CHANGING THE COIFFURE

I parted my hair on the opposite side
to see if this change would affect my attitude
the ooronavirus/Trumpian reign had birthed —
one affecting my country 'tis not of me,
and the attitude kept trying to pop back in place
where once had been strands of sanity,
resistance, insistence against changed direction
that only matched my vanity.

CORONA ISOLATION

When isolated she should be
somewhere she likes a lot
instead of in a place that she does not.

CRITICAL THINKING

Distraction isn't the same
as stimulation,
it's like refusing the cup
and doing intinction...
if you'll pardon the religious distinction.

A DREAM

She came out of my past,
a woman who willed her grandchildren to me
and for whom I made eggs, bacon, grits:
food she would have cooked
but said she was sick,
sick and tired of serving her family
so I did this meal for them
and, in turn, they painted a table
not large enough to hold meals
but looked good, a f...-you gift
while she lay down and died.
No one cared except me,
except the empty space
that had held all her meals
and the way she cared for them.

CATERPILLAR

Rain falls on red and yellow blooms
we planted for my gray interior life —
something that persists
in awareness and sleep.
This morning the fog hovers
over a window box of oregano, basil,
herbs the wrens ignore,
favor a yellow green caterpillar
crawling on the ledge,
the solemn enquiry of a risk taker,
huge probing eyes fixed
on the approaching squish.

ST. FRANCIS

I'm not at all surprised
that St. Francis's tonsure has turned white
although he still stands erect
among fading flowers
during these end times,
an innocent in a corrupt country,
its citizens immersed in the god Stock Market
while little particles of disease
come out of people's mouths
to make more particles of disease
although the president says viruses
really don't exist except for Democrats.
However, he has lost his sense of smell,
a symptom of the dread disease
and he doesn't know he's rotting inside.
He says he's safe as long as he wears
his long red tie, a tie that lengthens
like Pinocchio's nose each time he lies,
which is moment by moment.
I would be afraid if I were him
that unseen hands would reach out,
pull that tie tight to strangle the last word
he always has to have.
Still, in my quiet garden
St. Francis hasn't moved an inch
but I thought I heard him say "Peace,"
this morning, even in the downpour,
although his white tonsure is now cracked.

WHAT ABOUT WALLS

How much can happen
within a house walled in
like some flat-roofed abodes I saw in Iran
where women peered through aqua gates,
their men claiming the enclosed
were more romantic in their hot chadors
than women showing their legs
like western women in the Isfahan bazaar
when the Shah was in power.
But no one ever asked the entrapped
if given the opportunity, they would...

THE BIRD

This bird we ordered to decorate our herb bed
has one aqua colored glass eye,
looks like a peacock
advertised as a heron;
he's now held down by two steel pegs
and surveys the yard
as if he's overlooking a lake.
I think he wishes grass was water
or we'd water the grass
so he could feel more at home
on this stony mountain plateau,
a half-sun glinting on his one glass eye
blinding him like a cataract.
I think he wishes he could remember
what life was like on a central Florida lake
and exactly how he lost his eye
now that he's become a fish out of water.

MORE ON THE NON-EXISTENT VIRUS

I'm allowed to sit on my porch,
to bask in Vitamin D on sunlit days,
to catch a ray of sunlight
and rub it into my cheeks,
a shield against the virus
that doesn't exist
except for people over 65
while young people die like flies
on the beaches, in the bars
sans masks, sans sense,
saying let granny sit in the sun
behind a fence and Is it tall enough?
Only we, the eternally young,
have immortality by the tail
where our brains have been re-located.

THE FAMILY BUSINESS

I wrote a short story "The Family Business,"
about the treachery of family businesses,
how one person either rises to the top
via corruption or no one gets to be the chief.
in my family, the case being the engine
of a Ford auto business that coughed and died,
the effects of envy, greed, and power madness
killing off the success
of one generation's vision and hard work.
Yesterday, a similar story came via the net
telling of corruption in another family business
now headed by a greedy witch
who has grabbed each unsuspecting member,
one by one, and put them in a heavily-scented
gingerbread house that she slowly eats.
My stomach hurt for my friend all day
but I kept my prolonged distance
from the wicked witch. I have no taste
for gingerbread and know a witch
when I see one, especially someone
who heads a family business
that she turns into straw...
for a broom now ablaze.

MINTING

I make it a point to sniff mint
at least once a day
when a summer wind
makes their leaves tremble
a sharp scent into the air
while I sit among the balm of seasonings
that challenge the non sequitur of clover
whose bouffant hairdos
have begun to blow awry.

MORE TRUMPETING ABOUT THE TWEETER

You'd think that by now
our enlightened religious bodies
having read the Gospel for years
and preaching about same
would have a clear picture
of Jesus in their minds,
his actions reflecting
all the fruits of the spirit:
Joy, peace, long suffering...
but that was St. Paul's list,
of course, and the trend now
is to imagine Jesus
overturning tables in the marketplace,
jeering at Martha because she cleaned house,
favoring an entire group of society
and judging another —
just a caricature of our worst impulses,
some guy we can get comfortable with
and excuse away bullying
until that activity becomes unpopular.
Today I read that there are those
who believe God sent Trump
as the anointed one
to show us the way,
in my mind, the way
to become a dying species
while eating hamburgers in bed.

SEWANEE

I named this place Gray-burg
after I'd been here a year,
sky overhead the color of slate,
the first of thirteen years I've lived here;
from the beginning, a depressing place
attracting clergy, wealthy students,
black gowns flapping in the breeze
of Academia and hierarchal religion,
snobbery clouding my liberal soul.
For awhile, I found a haven
among Anglican nuns
kneeling in their castle on the bluff —
that is, before the virus came;
and now that we can no longer
breathe holy air and tell our stories,
entertain Sisters at breakfast in the refectory
there's only this scent of an aging house
and a herb garden
mingling with the scent of snobbery,
so I lace up my vagabond shoes
and turn the pages of an Atlas
searching for a new place to belong
where the sun will beam on my old age.

A MOTHER/DAUGHTER CONVERSATION

Every morning my oldest daughter calls:
Louisiana to Tennessee,
no special bulletins transmitted,
just seeking exchange
from isolated parts of the world,
listening for changed momentum
in varying scales of monotony:
steep to swamp.
But who would know
the difference in terrain
except through voice variance,
one striving for ascending arpeggio,
the other a deeply descending alto,
Bach's Joy of Man Desiring
and Mozart's Requiem Mass
straining for daily harmony
in one dissonant symphony.

THE BENEFITS OF INSOMNIA

An insomniac misses sleep
but not an air show;
fireflies in the woods
blink on/off signals,
night predators rush out
sensing danger;
and, unaccustomed to entertainment,
clutch the night air
where sudden light has been.

BEGETTING IGNORANCE

Tribalism equals tribulation,
and along with environmental destruction
signals the end of civilization
someone predicted the other day.
Yes, herd mentality
and hard to say which is more toxic;
but from my experience watching tribes
at work and play,
I'd say tribes...
They are the hearts of no hearts
that sit on their porches of glowing hate
for those not in their tribe
and kiss each other's money.
I say go ahead and marry your sister,
foster more "special ones"
so the world can "end
not with a bang but a whimper."*
No blood letting,
just Blood begetting ...Blood...
a family motto that makes my own run cold.

*From "The Hollow Men" by T. S. Eliot

THE EFFECTS OF UNABLE TO TRAVEL

After completing a book of poetry
entitled *We Vagabonds*,
it's natural to ponder
how doing without travel
charges vagabond yearnings
in those who suffer from wanderlust,
how the mere sight of a train
racing the track at Cowan, Tennessee
excites the car we're riding in,
the engine continuing to hum
and would accelerate
if the lever wasn't stuck in "Park."
Imagine how our heart's desire
for the open road,
higher and lower elevations,
back paths and long highways
could cause sudden propulsion —
no matter the direction, East or West —
the car abruptly leaping into the air
and moving into an open box car...
traveling fast.

THAT GREEN-EYED MONSTER

If you watch the movie "Paterson"
you'll see a huge ugly dog shred
a bus driver's journal of poems
he has crafted while driving
through Paterson, New Jersey daily;
this canine exhibits violent jealousy
because he's left alone at home
while the bus driver and wife
take a pleasant day off without him.
And you can't help wanting to send
the big-jawed, ugly animal
to a shelter
where there aren't any poets
or any reasons to write poetry
among a herd of flea-bitten castaways
who, perhaps have betrayed their masters
by destroying their lifework.
But the story doesn't end there
because the bus driving poet
writes journal after journal of poems
that make him famous worldwide
and the dog develops severe bruxism —
"serves him right."

THE LITTLE PEOPLE

Twenty thousand Cherokees rounded up,
put in stockades, then marched
on the Trail of Tears to Oklahoma;
half of them died along the way
a few hid in the mountains
near Sylva, North Carolina,
some just turned around
and went back, may have been
helped by the Little People.
Little People rumored to be two feet tall
but you can't see them
unless they want you to see them,
immortals, the Cherokee say,
you can hear them but can't see them,
although they are rumored
to have red whiskers, Dr. Spock ears
and squinty eyes,
live in tunnels and appear
by the light of the moon,
They aren't as mischievous as touted to be
but act as protectors who spread
the good news about Jesus.
When they first heard about
how he died, they wept.
And wherever their small tears
fell to the ground,
the tears became fairy crosses.
You can buy these in souvenir shops
in Sylva, but if you purchase one,
next morning don't look under your porch steps.

LIFT UP YOUR VOICE

No answer when someone yells at the sky,
'seems the force of rain only strengthens
when it hears a hysterical voice,
shaking fists at the heavens won't help either
except in the case of Scarlet O'Hara
in the movie, "Gone With the Wind"
after the Yanks have pillaged Tara
and she finds and eats a raw turnip.
or was it a radish?
Some satisfaction comes from bellowing,
lungs expanding, noise exploding
two days away from the 4th of July.
Perhaps our forefathers raised their voices
in such a manner when they gave up
the tyranny of The Crown
and began expanding the country
by expanding their lungs,
whatever the cause for yelling,
there are now countrywide contests
for such a boisterous activity
but there isn't much respect
for someone who boasts
"Nobody ever heard me
raise my voice to anyone."

BATH WATER

When your offspring get depressed,
try this standard line from
an experienced mom's book
of enduring advice:
Fill a tub (not a shower
and preferably an ancient claw foot
one in your grandmother's house
(if you happen to have inherited it)
with as much hot water
as your tender skin can withstand,
particularly if you are of southern
Scots/English descent and
are one of the "pink people."
Submerge your entire body,
sans face, for one half hour
without soaping, scrubbing
or even thinking of getting clean.
Meditate on the amniotic fluid
in which you once floated
and release the thoughts
of the storm that ejected you
into this heavily-burdened world,
then think how much better off
you are than, say, skunks,
beasts with white stripes or otherwise,
who have no one to keep them company.
and no reason to bathe.

ELEPHANT EARS

Those giant green ears need water
and if not given a drink
have been heard, through ultrasound,
to scream their neglect,
die of thirst.
However, some have been known
to reach 20 ft. heights
with five ft. long, 4 ft. wide heads
resembling beach umbrellas;
Jungle umbrellas
where tigers claim shade,
stretch out and sip
lime-colored margaritas
drunk before noon,
at dusk, hangovers on the prowl.

ABOUT DOLDRUMS

Doldrums.
Take that word apart
and you can hear a doll drumming —
perhaps a Patsy Ann wooden doll
like the one your mother gave you
for Christmas back in the forties
before doll makers made any claims
for creating dolls that looked authentic.
Doldrums — Patsy Ann making rapid taps
that built into a rumble,
brought down your mood
with a clash of cymbal,
ended your imaginary tea party.
And, in the face of a new sibling
screaming for care in the night
you didn't want one of those babies
to be real anyway.
Thus, doldrums,
best left in the toy chest.

ARIAS

Open the back door
and step outdoors.
What has been silent
becomes birds singing —
they know us on sight
or by step, even mumbled utterances,
and their songs may be the same
even if the territory is different:
"You're something to sing about,"
they chirp, at least they think so
even if our fellow humans
have devolved to the point
of mistrust and hate
and the only songs they sing
are ones of censor.
What if we listened to those birds,
practiced the same arpeggios?
Would we develop voices
that carried on the air
far enough to invite praises
rather than pusillanimity,
overcame such a large
and inharmonious word?

ABOUT HELL

The world will soon burn up
today's headlines insinuate.
Hell really is close
and now we've gone and done it
despite the view of Liberals
who say there is no hell.
Here it is,
it's been there all along
farther back than Dante's inferno,
farther back than Satan
in the Garden of Paradise
farther, even, than Creation's bang
which was really the echo of Ending.
It's July 4th
and you can hear It exploding —
not just an aimless prediction —
it's the noise of extinction.
So you think you're independent?
You can't make a fire extinguisher
large enough...

HAIRLOOMS

There's enough hair to go around
since the pandemic struck
and all beauty shops closed.
Actually, there's more than enough
passed on from former generations —
long, straight white hair
framing time-wrinkled faces,
more to wash, hard to groom
looms and looms of hair,
strands left on clean pillows,
carpets, dishes, chairs,
snowy antimacassars created
without crocheting a stitch.

JUDGEMENT ON NOT BEING JOYOUS

There's always a judgement
coming from someone I call
"Happy Little Wash Day Song"
who posts happy notes on facebook,
a person who attempts to shame
anyone who complains
about anything at all.
You should be happy, she says,
look at my smile
and read salubrious words
I utter every other breath.
She's trying to convince everyone
that nothing unfortunate ever happens,
this Pollyanna reborn in anti-tragedian ardor.
Think of women who used
to enjoy washing clothes, she touts,
scrubbing on washboards
or turning the crank of wringer machines
singing happy little wash day songs,
hovering over water that fills three tubs:
one for soaping,
one for bluing (I know not what or why)
one for clear water rinse.
Of course, they graduated to wringer machines
like the one the two year old next door
put her arm through
and, finally, the Beloved Bendix
our friend grudgingly admitted might become
a happy little wash day song
but, then again, it might hinder
the effectiveness of happy little wash days
of old and she'd never be able
to judge and chide people
who showed long faces

when misfortune struck.
It was her mission in life, you see.
You can look her up on facebook
the unhappiest happy face there,
gritting her teeth and flashing
a phony smile over a large basket
of dirty laundry.

ISAAC

Yesterday's sermon delivered
in a sophisticated cathedral in
New York City was all about Abraham
at 100 years of age getting it up
to fertilize one of Sarah's ancient eggs,
her laughing all the while
he was carrying on with uncommon verve
until her stomach swelled up with child
and she felt something stir with life,
The point of it all was that God
can do anything, create a miracle
of childbearing in old age,
everyone laughing their way through it
even naming the son born of that union
Isaac, which means laughter
like we're doing now
at this God-inspired work
accomplished without one grain of Viagra.

DESERT IMAGES

One of my favorite books
is a wood-covered volume
formerly marked DISCARD;
I rescued when I worked at a public library.
It's titled Plants of Sun and Sand
published by the Governor's Office
Tucson, Arizona, circa 1939.
I love this record of desert plants,
the struggle for existence
among cacti, candleflowers, saltbush,
mesquite, all the sun and sand growth
Zane Grey described in his western tales,
(and he was one who loved describing).
They could have been plants of this place
where 1/13th of the world's cacti grows;
and my favorite is the mesquite
with its spidery limbs,
home of the Pack Rat band,
members of which will steal and hide
your Grandmother's prized silver spoons
then gift you with something
they've stolen during a chollo raid,
You know, that honor among thieves
kind of thing —
perhaps a packet of Mormon Tea
used to treat venereal disease,
but an unfair exchange
if you don't have any need to drink it.

FALSE ADVERTISING

An ad for a tiny house village,
scaled down residences
only a few miles down the road from us:
two bedrooms, two baths,
studio and a patio,
1000 ft. of luxury living
decorated close quarters;
an attractive ad compelling us
to drive to Tracy City
and view this attraction,
twice passing a large wood,
miles of undeveloped land
devoid of any activity
except wildlife, houses so tiny
we couldn't see them at all.

GRAMMAR

I am reading about the efficacy
of nouns in a world that values verbs —
things that move around causing disarray
until a noun comes along
and pins everything down temporarily;
but never use an adverb (as above)
because the verb has already done
what was necessary to do.
Strunk and White say
if you don't use them
while conversing with others
don't use them at all,
adding "ly" to words is like
"putting a hat on a horse"
or a stickpin in a tie?

IVY

Ivy crawls on outer walls
always looks like its growing
on the wrong thing,
tentacles curled around window sills;
makes no categorical decisions
about its home base,
enters any surface it touches
and makes offers for life support
it really doesn't provide.

HEAVEN

If you believe in heaven
it's going to be a lot like coronavirus,
no touching, no seeing friends,
not even speaking, just memories
like the Christian Scientists believe,
you know, thoughts wandering among clouds,
the high life of inspiritedness,
even on stormy days
when tornados twist,
tsunamis stir —
any abruption, interruption —
you're going to be above it all.

YOU GOT THIS

I write in a journal
labeled "You Got This,"
gift from a friend and supporter
of my daily scribblings
but I haven't determined
what "this" is
or the word "it" for that matter
but I do remember
going through EST
back in the eighties
and exclaiming with 200 others
at the training's finish,
"*This* is *it*,"
both words I've tried to define —
"this" and "it,"
and coming up with
"that which is,"
not much better, that is...

FRETTING

shows itself at night,
stars fall,
blood streaks the moon,
will there be a tomorrow?
Did I inherit this worry, worry
from Grandmother Nell,
a ghost ship sailing on still waters?
Did I create a deserted warehouse
where there are no broken windows?
Fuss, fuss, fuss
I used to say about Grandmother Nell
as she pedaled an ancient Singer,
stitched her worries into my thin skin,
passed on her home-sewn smock,
deep pockets filled with allergies to sunlight.

MERCADO

When I parted my hair
back to the right side
what arose to consciousness
was a curious phenomenon —
that of Mercado, the genderless icon
of Puerto Rico who wooed millions
with his horoscope, an instrument
that could see far
into galaxies of the future.
This mad star from another world.
was brought here
on the dust of other planets
wearing heavy glittering cloaks
large sparkling rings on his hands,
a superhero holding out his arms,
believing himself to be
a vessel of gods that used to be
and launching a sky of stars
surrounded by smoke.
But he got to the bottom of things,
all the while promising
that he'd do people's believing
for them, transport them
with symbols and sequins...
pulled the wool over millions of eyes
while he applied mascara to his false ones.

THIS BOX TURTLE

lived in sewage tunnels of New York City
before finding her way to The Mountain,
something written on her back —
Egyptian or Farsi —
words of a different shape
and yellow in color.
She must have lived in the mideastern sector
of the City as she now searches
for remains from a heaping plate
of *chelow kebab* or *fesenjan*
(sparrows fried in pomegranate juice),
wonders if life here is more difficult
crouched in my yard
under the hose connection that leaks
than it is in the canals beneath the Big Apple.
She seems to be hoping
something might happen
to restore her bellicose disposition
so she can make her way back to the City;
until then, here she sits,
sticking her neck out again,
and again, musing that if she leaves
she has to pass through Louisiana
where 30,000 of her kind
are being captured and exported yearly.
It is written that she can live 100 years
and I'm hoping she moves on,
if she has attained the century mark;
picture her remembering her youth
and rearing up one morning
with rouged feet doing the Lindy Hop,
a 1920's flapper hiding in my garden hose
and if I turned on the faucet...

TENDING THE GARDEN

Botanists don't know what to do
with cultivated gardens,
they prefer to hunt tall weeds
growing in unkempt fields,
places with No Trespassing signs
or along busy Interstate highways
where it isn't feasible to back up
and pluck roadside plants,
but if they see a dirty white weed
like *Eupatorium Capillifolium*
the car behind you is a goner.
For botanists, a planted garden
is much too much trouble —
digging, seeding, watering,
dodging bees, wasps,
and poison ivy tentacles,
waiting, waiting, for blooms
and finally leaping with joy
when they glimpse those tall weeds
to which they're so inured
spring up and take over anyway.

THUNDERSTORMS

"The way you weather thunderstorms
is important," Grandmother Nell always said.
She saw a Baptist minister struck down
by a lightning bolt at a church gate,
the image forever etched in her mind.
If we were visiting during a thunderstorm
we had to "get up in the bed," she'd say,
"mattresses will protect you from strikes."
So we'd gather — as many grandchildren
as had come to visit, maybe five of us
and, of course, herself;
windows firmly shut,
electrical devices unplugged,
we'd sit during a humid afternoon,
sweaty body to sweaty body
sweltering for an hour or so,
sometimes two,
while the storm raged outside.
Finally, when we had reached
the point of suffocation,
she released us, danger gone,
one more summer day's reprieve,
the weather vane of mattress
turned over (but never aired).
My grandfather, returning from
his business selling Ford motor cars,
would say, "Nell, you do know
there's lightning attraction
in those steel coil springs
beneath that lumpy mattress?"
And she'd say:
"Everything in this world is layered...
we just have to get in between when we can."
???

COOKIES

If there's one addiction I could develop
it would be that of cookie consumption,
that is, if most of them didn't make me ill
and kickstart severe allergies;
However, vanilla Oreos
top the list of tolerations
and I could consume a package a day
but restrict the package to two days
just to fool myself into thinking
I'm not a cookie hog.
I could do equal damage to
entire cakes, pies, ice cream
and the like but I'm allergic to dairy
and suspect that sugar intolerance
is creeping up, could take over
any moment and even dark chocolate
is running a good race with cookies.
I know that Ovid said we're always
"striving after what is forbidden and
coveting what is denied us,"
and he was a misunderstood literary genius,
however he was referring to adultery
rather than cookies
unless a good looking one walked by...

FOG

isn't just a feature of British mysteries
based in London
or in the murky Louisiana marshlands,
it also hovers over The Mountain
at Sewanee, over the Entitled
Privileged, and Of the Manor Born
now sequestered just like the *hoi*

polloi living in the rest of the world.
These entitled beings have attempted
to hide the truth in the swirling mist
that breaks up and descends to the valley
where common people reside —
the truth being a few words
about those of us who,
during the 40's and 50's,
developed a formula called Greatness.
And that's what the entire world
called our generation — The Great Ones,
meaning the USA, its government,
its people, its dogs and cats,
birds and butterflies,
anyone who set foot here
(and anyone could set foot here then)
who pledged to practice two things:
generosity and integrity.
If I say any more, I'll be accused
of moving from preaching to meddling
an old southern maxim I try
to keep in mind when down and dirty
is going on.
Now that the fog has lifted
I can reveal to you
that Happy Little Wash Day
of several doodle poems back

may not like this pronouncement
about our generation,
but, again, the truth is the truth,
and poor unenlightened woman
who has to keep up her reputation
as a happy little wash day song
really doesn't know a thing
about taking care of dirty laundry —
how to stir up a good tub of suds.

ANOTHER GOING TO DIDDY WAH DIDDY FROM THE OTHER SIDE

I look at the postcards again:
scenes of the Southwest Mother collected
while we "gypsied,"which is what my father called
the family odyssey to Diddy Wah Diddy—
California to you —
a place where the sky is biggest,
the desert hottest and endless.
Every summer I suffer from longings
for another carefree singular-journey
like the one that ended with a turnaround
in congested L.A. traffic
that had taken my family deep into
the heart of life without bathrooms,
all night riding through hot deserts
and sleeping on state park tables,
all the discomforts
of travel without destination.
I've always wondered about
what might have happened
if we hadn't turned around
and returned to the Deep South.
Would I still be wandering?
At some point toward the end
of that odyssey, Mother wrote
on a postcard she had collected,
one bearing a photograph
of Brownwood, Texas (?)
and addressed to someone not living
at the address to which she never sent it:
"We are not too fond of California
except to look at."
Obviously, she had gypsied enough in her
"quaint caravan" but she did leave me

with the postcard collection
and forever yearnings to purchase an RV —
towable, motorized, specialty, park model,
anything with a pack on its back,
and, today, from the other side
I heard her plaintive cry:
"Sell your Roomba. Shake the dust, baby."